HOME ALONE

Barbara Nascimbeni

Every morning when she leaves,

she says, 'Be a good dog,

my FRI-FROU-sweetheart,

don't worry, the day will go by very fast.'

I'm not FRI-FROU, nor FRI-FRI,
or FROU-FROU-sweetheart,
I'm FRIDO,
and she is my owner.

But when I'm finally home alone…

I love to ride her scooter.

Watch me go!

WHEEE!

Ouch...

Crashing about is hard work.
Hmmm, her bed looks
warm and soft.

So warm, so soft…

…and so bouncy!
Up!
And down!

Over and over…

Until I am worn out.

When I'm home alone,
I like to take a peek in the fridge.

YOGHURT

HAM

CHEESE

BUTTER

MILK

WINE

RASPBERRY JUICE

SALAMI

BUTTER

MUSTARD

BREAD

I can make myself
a sandwich with butter,
salami and mustard.

I LOVE mustard. I think…

Perhaps I don't like mustard.

When I'm home alone, I like to watch TV…

The yoga show is my favourite.

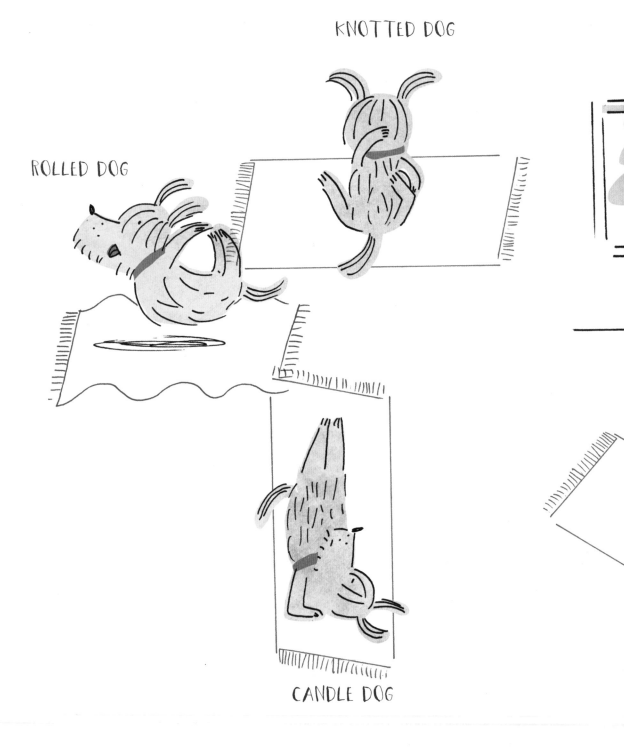

KNOTTED DOG

ROLLED DOG

CANDLE DOG

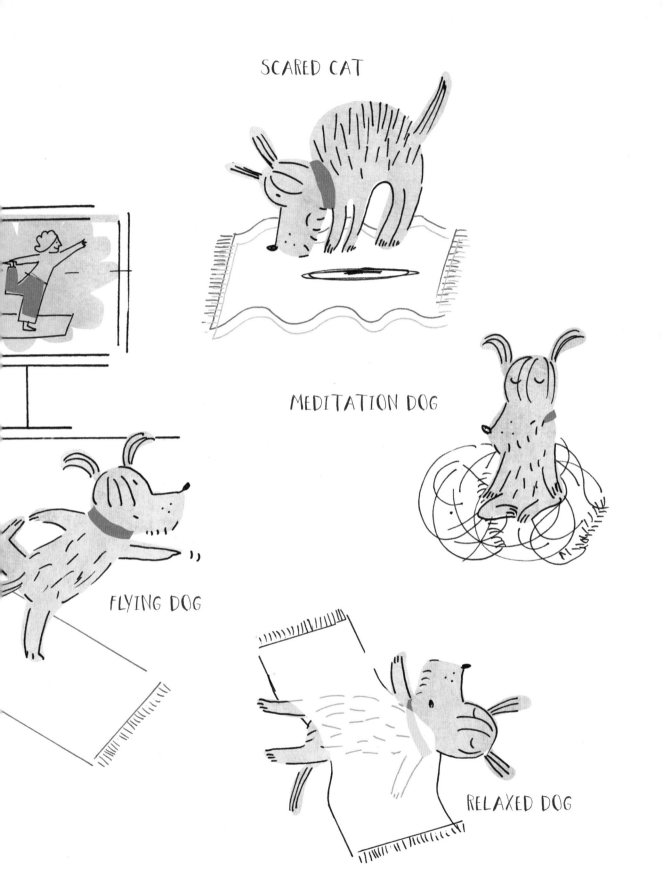

SCARED CAT

MEDITATION DOG

FLYING DOG

RELAXED DOG

When I'm home alone, I like to use the
computer to talk to my friends.
They tell me all the news.

When I'm home alone,
I love to open up the big wardrobe
and look at all her clothes…

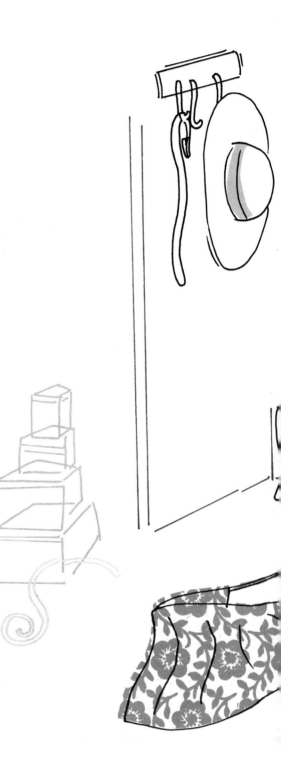

I know her favourite shoes,

her favourite hat,

her favourite glasses,

her favourite scarf.

She has very good taste.

DING
DONG!

Sometimes I forget I've invited my best friends over.
Lola lives in the house next door,
and Rudi lives on the streets.

Time for some music!

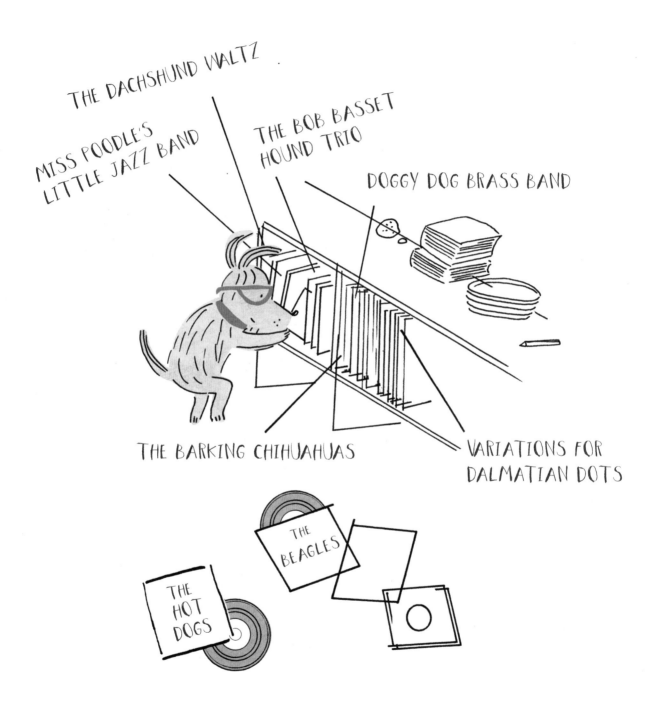

We listen to her favourite records.
Rudi and Lola love them.

We do crazy dancing!

Then, I play a concert for them.

I can play really well.

Then I'm alone again – at last!

I know how to order pizza – with sausage.

And then, I like to relax and read magazines.

Yikes! She'll be back soon.

She doesn't have to know that I like…

her warm, soft bed,

salami and mustard sandwiches,

to try on her clothes,

to ride on her scooter,

to go on her computer,

to play her records,

to read her magazines,

to watch TV...

Thank goodness I cleaned up.

I've been here all day.

DING DONG

When I'm home alone, she knows that
her FRI-FROU-sweetheart is the sweetest of all dogs!

For Gisela

With thanks to Françoise Gerbaulet and Ruth Redford

First published in the United Kingdom in 2021 by
Thames & Hudson Ltd, 181A High Holborn, London WC1V 7QX

Home Alone © 2021 Thames & Hudson Ltd, London
Text and Illustrations © 2021 Barbara Nascimbeni

Copyedited by Ruth Redford

British Library Cataloguing-in-Publication Data
A catalogue record for this book is available from the British Library

ISBN 978-0-500-65261-9

Printed and bound in China by C & C Offset Printing Co. Ltd

MIX
Paper from
responsible sources
FSC® C008047
www.fsc.org

Be the first to know about our new releases,
exclusive content and author events by visiting
thamesandhudson.com
thamesandhudsonusa.com
thamesandhudson.com.au